Pearl's Dressing-Up Dreams

The Picnic Basket

JENNY OLDFIELD

Illustrated by Dawn Apperley

Hodder Children's Books
A division of Hachette Children's Books
338 Euston Rd, London NW1 3BH
An Hachette UK company
www.hachette.co.uk

"I met a very friendly rat," Pearl told Amber and Lily.

"Eww!" Lily turned up her nose.

"Rats are nasty, dirty things," Amber said.

"This one wasn't," Pearl insisted. "He was kind to me when the Duke threw me in the dungeon. He brought me something to eat."

Amber sat on the big wooden box in her basement. "I feel sorry for you, Pearl. This dressing-up thing isn't working out, is it?"

"There are no princes in Red Riding-Hood world," Lily sighed.

"No fairy godmothers," Amber added. "Only talking rats and squirrels and stuff, plus the Wolf, of course."

"I love it!" Pearl protested. "I want to go back." For days now she'd been coming to Amber's basement and trying on things from the dressing-up box. So far nothing had whooshed her back into the fairy tale. "OK, so it's not Cinderella and it's not Snow White, but it is magic, believe me!"

Lily and Amber shrugged. "If you say so," Lily muttered. "But we worry about you when you whoosh off. We keep

4

thinking the Wolf has got you!"

"'Grandmamma, what big teeth you have!'" Amber pretended to snarl and snap at Pearl. "'Wrraaagh!'"

Pearl ignored her. "Get off the box and let me look inside," she insisted. "There must be something magic to take me back."

So Amber gave in and opened the dressing-up box, watching Pearl begin to sort through the dresses, hats and shoes. "No good," she muttered, throwing a frilled petticoat to one side.

Soon they all were diving into the box.

"How about this?" Amber held up a cat costume she'd once worn for a school play – a black leotard with a cardboard cat-mask minus one ear and its whiskers.

"Tried it," Pearl replied. "It didn't work."

"Or this?" Lily held up one of Amber's mum's old party dresses – purple and slinky with silver sequins.

"Tried it," Pearl muttered. "And these red shoes, and this pashmona . . ."

"Pash*mina*," Lily corrected. "Hey, let me see – I really like that!"

Lily wrapped the soft cream shawl around her shoulders, while Amber slipped her feet into the red high-heeled shoes. Then they pranced around the basement playing princesses. "Greetings, Your Majesty!" "Charmed to meet you, Your Highness!" Curtsey and bow, totter and giggle.

"This is serious!" Pearl tutted as she carried on searching. "I keep thinking about the stag. I bet Wolfie's still stalking

him. And then there's the Duke and his hunters to worry about."

Pearl had reached the very bottom of the dressing-up box. Her fingers closed around the handle of a square wicker basket and she pulled it out. "What's this?" she asked Amber.

"That old thing? It's the picnic basket we used to take on holidays to France."

"It's still got all the plates and stuff

inside," Pearl said, lifting the wonky lid. The basket was lined with green checked cloth. There were plastic knives and forks, green plastic plates and . . . what was that strange light coming from inside?

"Uh-oh!" Lily and Amber gasped.

The lid was open and the light out. It filled the basement, growing brighter and brighter, whooshing into every corner.

Pearl almost dropped the picnic basket. She was dazzled by the light, her heart began to beat faster. *This is it!* she thought. *Here we go again!*

It was like swimming without water – floating in thin air! Pearl clutched the basket and let the wind whirl her out of the basement in a bright white light, making her dizzy, whooshing over hills and mountains, down into the meadow close to Red Riding-Hood's cottage. *Bump!*

She landed in a field full of daises and buttercups, staring up at Hans, the boy next door.

2

"Hello, Red Riding-Hood – where did you spring from?" Hans asked.

"Erm – er – ummm."

"You weren't here when I last looked. What are you doing, hiding in the long grass and making people jump?"

Pearl stood up and brushed herself down. "I've been here all the time," she fibbed. "It's you, Hans – you should look where you're going."

"Oh, Little Miss Prim and Proper, just like your gran, ever since she started working for the Duchess!"

"What about Gran?" Pearl was glad to change the subject. Still holding tight to the picnic basket, she strolled with Hans towards home.

Hans laughed. "I saw her just now. She brought the Duchess's baby to play on the green. What's happened to her voice?"

Pearl shrugged. Of course, she hadn't seen her Red Riding-Hood grandma for days. "I don't know what you mean."

"'My good man this, my good man that!'" Hans mimicked a hoity-toity voice. "It sounds like she's swallowed a pebble!"

"Oh."

"Lah-di-dah, just because she's working at the castle. She forgets she's still no better than the rest of us."

"You know what she's like," Pearl said awkwardly. She stumbled and almost dropped the basket, letting the lid fall open and the contents spill out.

"What's this?" Hans cried, picking up a plastic knife. "Yes, I know it's a knife, but what's it made of? I never saw anything like this before."

"Oh, it's just some old thing," Pearl muttered. How did you explain plastic when it hadn't been invented yet?

"Blunt as anything!" Hans scoffed, trying the blade across his palm. "And look at that basket – it's dropping to pieces."

"So why don't you help me mend it?" Pearl swung the subject around once more. They'd reached the cottage and seen Hans's father unloading a cartful of logs for Pearl's mother. In the distance, Pearl's grandmother was still playing with Max, the baby from the castle.

"Yoo-hoo!" the old lady called when she spotted Pearl. "There you are, Red Riding-Hood. And you, my good boy!" she shouted to Hans. "I wonder if you could spare a moment of your time!"

Hans's eyebrows shot up. "What did I tell you?" he muttered out of the corner of his mouth. "Lady Muck!"

"Yoo-hoo, yoo-hoo!" Gran called as Hans grabbed the picnic basket and made his getaway. "Come back, young man. I

13

have an errand for you to run. Are you deaf? Why, Red Riding-Hood, you'll have to do the job instead!"

"I need you to run up to the castle," Red Riding-Hood's grandmamma said in a slow, sing-song voice. "I have forgotten the baby's bonnet and the sun comes down very strong on his head."

Pearl swallowed hard, trying not to laugh at Gran's posh new voice. "Where shall I look for it?"

"In His Baby Grace's nursery. I left it by his cot. Run quickly, my dear, or else poor Max will get sunburned." With a queenly wave of her hand, the old lady dismissed Pearl and turned her attention to Max.

So Pearl sped off along the village street,

past Farmer Meade's milking parlour, up the steep hill towards the castle.

This is hot work! Pearl said to herself as she arrived at the castle, caught her breath then knocked on the main door.

Rat-a-tat-tat!

"Yes?" a proud footman inquired through a grille.

"I've come for Max's hat," she said breathlessly. She didn't like being near the castle. It reminded her of being slung in the dungeon with only the rat to talk to. "It's in the nursery, near the cot."

"And you expect me to run and fetch it?" the footman sneered, the gold braid on his purple uniform glinting in the sun.

"My job is to serve the Duke and Duchess, not to run errands for a village girl!"

"Then I'll get it myself," Pearl sighed, waiting for the door to open. She ran across the courtyard to the sound of arguing from above.

"*Why* must you go out hunting every day?" the Duchess whined. "Why can't you stay and keep your wife company instead?"

"And why must I answer these questions?" her husband retorted. "I hunt because I am a duke and I do as I like. Besides, the bark of the hunting hounds is better than your voice nagging me from dawn to dusk."

"Aahhh!" the Duchess cried, flinging herself out of the room and crashing into

16

Pearl on the wide stone staircase. "Those cruel words strike me to the heart. I will lock myself in my chamber and cry myself to death!"

"Oops, sorry!" Pearl mumbled as the purple Duchess bumped into her.

Luckily the grand lady was too upset to notice. Otherwise, it would have meant another trip to the dungeon for Pearl.

"Boo-hoo!" the Duchess cried as she slammed doors and shed crocodile tears.

Pearl took a deep breath then tiptoed past the Duke's chamber.

"Fetch my boots!" the Duke yelled from inside the room. "You out there in the corridor, fetch me my cloak and hat. I am going hunting!"

As if by magic the snooty footman

appeared with the Duke's garments.

He pushed Pearl out of the way to obey the order.

"*Oof!*" Pearl fell to her knees. She stumbled on down the corridor, glad when she reached the nursery and could nip in to find Max's sun hat.

But it wasn't next to the cot as her grandmother had said, nor on the floor beneath. Pearl searched everywhere. In the end she had to grab the closest thing to a baby's bonnet – a pillow case from the cot – and with her heart in her mouth she made her escape.

3

"A pillow case!" Pearl's grandmother exclaimed. "His Baby Grace can't wear a pillow case on his head! What were you thinking, Red Riding-Hood?"

"It was all I could find." Pearl took the offending item back. "The Duke and Duchess were having a fight. I got out as fast as I could."

"Tut-tut!" Searching in her apron pocket,

Gran dug out Max's bonnet. "Here it is. It was here all the time, after all!"

Doh! Pearl ground her teeth as her gran put the bonnet on the baby's head. She was glad when her mother came out of the cottage on to the village green, carrying Tommy.

"There, Baby Grace – the sun can't burn your cheeks now!" Gran cooed.

Max made a bad-tempered face.

"Here's Tommy to play with Max," Pearl's mum announced, putting the baby down on the grass.

Like Max, Tommy was crawling and taking his first tottery steps.

"Oh, my!" Gran snatched Max up from the blanket he'd been sitting on. "His Baby Grace can't play with a common child from the village. Whatever would Her Grace the Duchess say?"

Pearl's mum frowned. "Stop that at once, Mother."

"Stop what?" Gran asked, rocking Max in her arms.

Max wriggled and struggled to be let down.

"Drop your ridiculous airs and graces. It's me you're talking to, remember?"

"Oh – you're right, my dear. I'm sorry," Gran admitted as she lowered Max on to the blanket. "I'm getting too big for my boots, aren't I?"

"Yes! But I forgive you. Come here, Mother!" Pearl's mum laughed, and the two women hugged.

Meanwhile, Max crawled off the

blanket, trying to catch up with Tommy. "Goo! Goo!" the babies gurgled.

"Keep an eye on them, Red Riding-Hood. Your grandmother and I are going into the cottage for a nice cup of tea."

So Pearl minded the babies in the afternoon sun. She followed them as they crawled and toddled towards the duck pond.

Quack! the brown ducks said, swimming in circles at the edge of the pond. "Take care, Red Riding-Hood. The water's deep!" *Quack!*

So Pearl steered Tommy and Max back towards the swing, where a blackbird sang and a green woodpecker pecked at the bark, looking for insects.

Tap-tap-tock! The bird was busy, his long beak stabbing the trunk.

Ta-rum, ta-rum, ta-rum!

"Watch out!" the blackbird cried, fluttering up from his branch. "The Duke and his hunters are riding out!"

Ta-rum! The hunters' horn sounded

louder. Their hounds barked and loped down the hill.

"They're galloping this way!" the blackbird warned as he flew high in the air. "Beware, Red Riding-Hood – the huntsmen will not stop for love nor money!"

With a gasp Pearl heard the thunder of hooves coming down the hillside. She heard the baying of the Duke's hounds.

"Max, Tommy, come here!" Pearl cried. She didn't know which way to run or who to grab first.

Frightened by the horn, the babies opened their mouths and bawled. Pearl's grandmother and mother rushed to the door of the cottage, took in the scene and screamed.

"Save His Baby Grace!" Gran cried, wringing her hands.

The hunters were already in sight, clattering down the village street, overturning Anna the milkmaid's churns and trampling Lydia's flowers.

"Tommy!" Pearl's mother darted towards her baby and held him close.

Still the Duke and his hunters charged and blew their horn. The hounds bounded on to the green.

As Pearl's mother ran to scoop Tommy from harm's way, Pearl rushed towards Max.

"Waaaghhh!" Max cried as horses, hounds and riders thundered towards him.

Pearl ran across their path, bent down

and picked up Max. She sprinted for the oak tree and pressed herself against it.

"Well done, Red Riding-Hood!" the woodpecker sighed.

"Brave girl!" Two squirrels peered down from a high branch.

Ta-rum, ta-rum! The horn sounded and, without a backward glance, the Duke galloped on.

"The Duke didn't even recognise his own son!" Pearl told Hans afterwards.

Her grandmother had carried Max into their cottage and scrubbed him clean.

("Boo-hoo," cried Max.)

Then she'd straightened his bonnet and tied his blue ribbons.

("Goo!" said Max, cheering up again.)

"Time for me to take him back to the

castle." Gran had said hasty goodbyes.

Pearl had stood at the door with Tommy, waving them on their way.

"He and his men rampaged through the village without even caring who was in his way," Pearl complained. "He could have killed poor Max for all he knew!"

"That's the Duke," Hans agreed. He'd come to show Pearl how he'd mended her picnic basket with new leather hinges. "He doesn't care for either man or beast."

"That's another thing!" Pearl went on, taking the basket and tidying its contents. She tucked plates neatly into their pouches, knives and forks slotted in beside. "Why does the Duke have to hunt wild animals?"

"Why is the sky blue?" Hans shrugged.

"Why is the earth flat?"

"What harm did the stag ever do to him?" Pearl wondered. She remembered the Duke's face with its long, curled moustache as he'd stampeded across the green. There had been a nasty look in his eye.

"Forget it," Hans advised. "Are you pleased with the basket?"

Pearl nodded. "Tomorrow I'll fill it with food, and have a picnic in the wood," she decided. "You know – a few cookies, some scones with a little pot of jam. That sort of thing."

"Sounds tasty," Hans said, his mouth watering. "Will you go by yourself?"

"You can come too," she told him kindly. "And . . . and . . ." No other names came to mind, unless she included grown-ups like Lydia and Anna. But then the picnic wouldn't be so much fun.

"And Tommy?" Hans suggested.

She shook her head. "He's too little." There was a silence as she thought harder. "I know! Why don't I ask the squirrels and the rabbits? The birds too. Even the stag if we can find him."

Hans stared at Pearl, open-mouthed. "You plan to invite animals to your picnic?"

"Yes. Like in the teddy bears' picnic!"

He frowned and shook his head.

"'If you go down to the woods today, you're sure of a big surprise!'" Pearl trilled. "'If you go down to the woods today, you'll never believe your eyes! For every bear that ever there was, is gathered there for certain because . . .'"

Hans blinked. "Mad!" he muttered.

"' . . . today's the day the teddy bears have their pic-nic!'"

"This afternoon!" Pearl told four grey rabbits at the edge of the wood.

She'd got up early to find the animals.

"Will there be food?" the rabbits asked, twitching their noses. "At this picnic you talk about, what will there be to eat?"

Pearl tried to come up with a rabbit treat. "Lettuce sandwiches!" she suggested.

"Yum!" the rabbits said, scampering off to tell their friends. "We'll be there when the sun is level with the tip of the ash tree on the hill!"

"Let the stag know, but don't tell the Wolf!" Pearl shouted after them.

"You can trust us!" the rabbits promised, disappearing down their burrow.

"*Tu-whit* – what time? Where?" the owl asked. He yawned because he'd been up all night.

"This afternoon, when the sun is level

with the tip of the ash tree," Pearl replied. "We'll meet in the woodcutter's clearing."

"*Tu-whit* – too early for me!" the owl hooted. "I shall still be fast asleep!"

"I'll bring tasty sausage rolls," Pearl promised.

The owl blinked then stared. "Then I'll get up early and come to your picnic!" he promised, rising from his branch and flapping off slowly through the wood.

"Tell the stag if you see him. But don't let Wolfie find out!" Pearl called after him. "We don't want him spoiling our fun."

*

"Hazelnut cookies?" Pearl asked the squirrels clinging to the trunk of the sycamore tree. "Is that what you want me to pack in my picnic basket?"

"They're our favourite!" the squirrels chattered excitedly. "Sweet hazelnuts in crunchy biscuits. What could be better?"

"I'll make you some specially," Pearl agreed. She knew she ought to be getting back home to begin the baking if she were to be ready in time. "So you'll come?"

"Of course!" the young squirrels cried, scampering up into the branches, shaking the leaves as they played.

"And don't tell Wolfie!" she warned.

"Don't worry, we won't!" The youngest squirrel ran back down the trunk. "No one has seen the Wolf lately," he told Pearl.

"But the stag thinks he caught a glimpse of him yesterday – in the forest beyond the castle, over the far side of the hill."

"Good riddance – I hope Stag is right," Pearl said firmly. "And now I must go!"

The mist rose from the riverbank as Pearl hurried home. A pale sun sailed into view.

Ha-ha! Wolfie thought, lying low by the water's edge. He had travelled by night, keeping to the darkest shadows, to return to the meadow – his favourite hunting ground. *Let the fools believe that I am still far away. I will hide here amongst the roots of the old willow tree. I will lie low until the sun is level with the ash tree on the hill!*

For the Wolf had heard every word that Pearl had said to the rabbits, the owl and the squirrels. He had lurked behind trees and crept silently through the undergrowth. He had licked his lips.

"'If you go down to the woods today . . .'" Pearl hummed happily as she climbed the stile. She would need to make pastry for the sausage rolls and pick lettuces for the sandwiches. The fire must be lit and the oven heated. "'For every bear that ever there was . . .'"

Tender rabbits! Wolfie sighed, settling down to wait. *Tasty young squirrels and best of all . . .*

"'Today's the day the teddy bears have their pic-nic!'"

. . . Best of all will be juicy Little Red Riding-Hood, yum-yum!

5

"'If you go down to the woods today . . .'"
Pearl hummed. She rolled pastry for the
sausage rolls then checked the biscuits in
the oven.

"Hans left you a message," her mum
told her. "He said he'd meet you in the
clearing when the sun is level with the tip
of the ash tree. He might be a little late.
Does that make sense?"

"Yes thanks." Pearl hummed and rolled. "Did he say what he was doing before the picnic?"

"Helping his dad chop firewood at the far edge of the wood."

"Cool, thanks." Suddenly she looked up from her work. "Oh, bother!"

"What is it?" Pearl's mother began to butter bread for the lettuce sandwiches.

"I just remembered – there's someone I didn't invite." *My friend, the rat!* "He'll be upset when he finds out that we had a picnic without him."

"Who?" her mother asked, spreading the butter nice and thick.

"Someone at the castle." *Oh for a mobile phone!* Pearl thought. *A quick text in real life and the problem would be solved.* "I've probably got time to nip up there, if—"

"If I carry on getting the food ready here?" her mother guessed. She smiled. "Off you go, Red Riding Hood, and invite your friend to the picnic. I'll cope with the food, as long as Tommy stays asleep."

So Pearl put on her cloak and ran as fast as she could, up the hill, taking the wide steps to the castle two at a time and knocking hard on the door.

"Yes?" the proud footman said through the grille. He saw a small, breathless girl dressed in a long red cloak with the hood flung back.

"I have a message for the Duchess's

nursery maid, my Grandmamma!" Pearl gasped. "Please let me in!"

"You again." The grumpy footman opened the door. "Don't expect me to . . ."

"It's OK, I'll take the message myself," Pearl cut in. As usual, being at the castle made her feel nervous, so she hurried upstairs. "Gran, where are you? It's me – Red Riding-Hood!"

"Hush!" Gran warned, appearing at the nursery door. "His Baby Grace is sleeping!"

"Cool!" Pearl grabbed her grandmother by the hand. She spoke in a whisper. "That means you can show me where the key to the dungeon is kept!"

Her grandmother sailed down the corridor. "His Baby Grace is fast asleep," she told the chambermaids sweeping and dusting the stairs. "If he wakes, be sure to raise the alarm and run to find me."

"I need the dungeon key!" Pearl hissed again. "I have to be quick. Do you know where it is?"

"It's kept on a hook beside the suit of armour in the great hall," Gran said with a puzzled frown. "Why on earth should you want the key?"

Luckily for Pearl, just at that moment a chambermaid came running. "The noble baby is awake. He is crying!" she said.

"Oh, my! I am on my way!" Grandmamma cried. And, with a swish of her skirt, she turned and hurried off.

"By the suit of armour . . ." Pearl muttered, tiptoeing across the hall.

"Hanging on a hook . . ."

Yes, there it was – the key to the dungeons!

Pearl seized the key then ran down some stone steps and along a corridor to a stout wooden door. She put the key in the lock and turned it with trembling fingers.

She pushed the creaking door. She entered a dark tunnel with narrow doors leading off to the left and right. Cobwebs brushed her face. There was a *drip-drip* of water running down the slimy walls. *It's like the ghost train – seriously spooky!*

Whooo-ooo! A door blew open and a

42

wind gusted along the tunnel.

Where did that come from? Pearl wondered. She was about to turn and run when a small voice addressed her.

"Hello, stranger. What brings you here?"

"Who's that?" Pearl gasped.

"It's me. Look down, why don't you?"

In the darkness Pearl made out a pair of beady eyes. "Is that you, Rat?"

"Who else?" The rat sounded bored and grumpy. "This is where I live, isn't it? Anyway, Red Riding-Hood, what have you done wrong this time?"

"Nothing. I'm not in prison. I came because I wanted to."

"Huh!" Ratty led Pearl through some dirty puddles towards a narrow chink of light. "To what do I owe the pleasure of this visit then?"

Pearl gazed down at her sharp-featured friend. "I came to invite you to a picnic."

"A picnic – what's that?" Ratty asked.

"A party held in the open air, with food spread out on a nice clean tablecloth."

"In the open air, you say?" The rat preferred dark tunnels and the insides of drainpipes. He sounded doubtful about Pearl's invitation.

"Yes, I came specially to ask you. Don't worry – you'll be safe. There won't be any other humans there – except Hans."

"With food?" the rat inquired, twitching the tip of his nose.

"Yes. Whatever kind of food you like – cakes, biscuits, sandwiches."

"Bacon rind?" Ratty asked. "There's

nothing I like better than a nice crunchy strip of bacon rind."

"OK, I'll pack some in the picnic basket!" Pearl laughed. "So will you come?"

The rat sat back on his haunches. "When and where?" he asked.

Amongst the gnarled roots of the willow tree, Wolfie still lay. He was wide awake, watching and listening.

He saw Pearl leave her cottage and run up the hill. He saw her return.

Soon! he thought, one eye on the sun which was still high in the sky. *When the sun goes past its peak and begins to sink towards the ash tree on the hill, then the picnic will begin!*

6

"Lettuce sandwiches, sausage rolls, hazelnut cookies." Pearl listed some of the snacks she'd packed in the picnic basket. "And bacon rind – nice and crispy, just how Rat likes it!"

She was buzzing with excitement. Never in a million years would she have dreamed of holding this kind of a picnic with her woodland friends. "I hope I haven't forgotten anyone," she said quietly as she closed the lid. "And I hope Stag manages to come along."

Lifting the picnic basket from the table, she groaned at the weight. "Hea-vy!" she sighed. She put on her red cloak and left a note for her mum. "Back by sunset. Love Red Riding-Hood XXX"

As soon as Tommy had woken up, her mother had taken him to visit her sister, Gertie, and their cousin, Hannah, in the neighbouring village. "Have a lovely time!" she'd called to Pearl as she'd set off down the lane. "And don't eat too much!"

Pearl closed the front door and stepped out across the meadow, with the sun sinking past its midday peak and the shadows beginning to lengthen.

"Hello, Red Riding-Hood!" At the far side of the meadow, Farmer Meade rested on his pitchfork. "If you're off to visit your grandmamma, please pass on my best wishes!"

"I'm not. I'm going to have a picnic in the woods," Pearl told him cheerfully.

"She's a wonderful woman – your grandmother!" the red-faced farmer sighed. "The stuff of every man's dreams!"

Phut! Pearl puffed out her cheeks and hurried on. Gran might be like Superwoman, with her whirlwind energy and bossy ways, but Pearl had never thought of her as dream material.

"This hamper weighs a ton!" she sighed as she climbed the stile and entered the woods. "I'll be glad when I reach the clearing."

Plump and rosy, sweet and tender beneath that bright red cloak! Wolfie thought. He spied on Pearl through the long reeds that grew by the riverbank. His gleaming eyes followed her but he didn't move a muscle as she passed within a few metres of where he lay. *Delicious!*

Pearl lugged the picnic basket along the track. She could hear the *chop-chop-chop* of the woodcutter's axe. Hans and his father were still hard at work.

"Here comes Red Riding-Hood!" the young rabbits cried, hopping and bobbing. "We smell lettuce!"

"Right on time!" the squirrels chattered, scampering down from the branches. "Nuts, nuts, sweet hazelnuts!"

"You're late!" the rat grumbled at Pearl as she approached the clearing. He sat on a pile of logs, doing his best to look grumpy. But his nose twitched and his mouth curled up at the corners as he smelled the beautiful, crisp bacon rind inside her picnic basket.

"I'm not the least bit late!" she told

50

him. "You're early!"

She laid the hamper beside the logs. The animals gathered round as she opened the lid. Wonderful smells wafted up their nostrils.

"*Woo-woo*-where are the sausage rolls?" Owl asked as he swooped down from the branches of the tall ash tree.

"Here!" Pearl said, laying them out on the tablecloth which she'd spread on the forest floor. "Who'd like a napkin?"

Before the question was out of her mouth, the animals fell on the food. Small paws grabbed, sharp teeth nibbled, sighs of delight sounded in the clearing.

"Scrumptious!" a squirrel said, his cheeks stuffed full as a hamster's.

"Heavenly!" one rabbit whispered to

another as his front teeth sank deep into a lettuce heart.

"*Woo*-wonderful!!" the owl cooed over his sausage roll.

"Not bad, I suppose," Rat muttered as he gobbled his bacon rind.

"What shall I try?" Pearl asked. "Or should I wait until Hans gets here?"

I wouldn't wait too long if I were you, Red Riding-Hood! Wolfie sneered to himself as he left his riverside lair. He crept stealthily through the trees, licking his lips.

The animals crunched and chomped on their treats. They neither saw nor heard the enemy approach.

"Tuck in before it's all gone," the rat

advised through a mouthful of crumbs.

Or before I pounce! Wolfie thought with a vicious smile.

Whizz! An arrow flew through the air and thudded into the ash tree trunk.

For a split second the squirrels and the rabbits, the owl and the rat froze.

Whizz-thud! A second arrow hit the tree.

And in a flash the animals were gone. Pearl jumped to her feet in time to see the stag come crashing through the wood with the Duke's hounds at his heels.

The magnificent creature bounded between the trees, trying to throw them off, but the dogs were gaining on him.

Wolfie lay low behind a thorn bush and cursed his luck. "Yet again!" he snarled. "I am robbed of my prey!"

"Run, Red Riding-Hood!" the stag cried as he saw Pearl standing in stunned amazement. "Danger is all around. Run home as fast as you can!"

But Pearl stood her ground. She yelled and waved her arms at the bloodthirsty hounds, and ran across the path of the Duke and his hunters as they galloped through the wood.

The dogs closed on the stag. More arrows whizzed and thudded. The Wolf rose from his hiding place and prepared to flee.

"Wolf ahead!" the Duke cried hoarsely, suddenly pulling his horse off course and charging after Wolfie.

The huntsmen reined their horses back. "Who do we follow – the stag or the Duke?" they cried in confusion.

The stag felt the breath of the hounds at his heels. He looked ahead and saw a steep hillock topped by thorn bushes with rugged rocks to either side and who-knew-what beyond. He paused.

"Kill the Wolf!" Duke Egbert was in a rage as usual. His men split in all directions as he drew an arrow from his quiver and took aim.

"Oh no, you don't!" Wolfie fled towards the river with the cries of the angry Duke ringing in his ears.

Whizz-thud! Whizz! Whizz! Arrows rained around Wolfie's head.

Pearl saw the stag hesitate by the steep hillock. "Jump!" she cried as the hounds got ready to pounce.

And so the stag took a mighty leap. He cleared the hill and left the hounds standing at its foot, baying and whining as their master hunted down the Wolf.

"Thank heavens!" Pearl sighed to see that Stag was safe.

But the disappointed dogs rounded on her. Baying noisily, they charged.

Now Pearl ran – away from their sharp teeth, into the path of a confused huntsman, ready with his bow and arrow.

"Here, Pepper! Here, Prince!" he yelled at the lead dogs, calling them to heel.

They obeyed and the whole pack followed, trampling through the undergrowth and knocking Pearl off balance in their rush.

Pearl stumbled against the hunter's black mare, which reared in fright as Pearl's arm caught in his loose rein.

"Clumsy fool!" the rider cried, dropping his weapon and struggling to stay in the saddle.

The frightened horse lunged forward and unseated her rider, dragging Pearl sideways. She clung to the horse's mane as she veered away through the trees. The solid trunks grew blurred and the green canopy overhead began to tilt. Then there was a mighty thud and Pearl lay still as death on the ground.

7

"I hit him!" the Duke cried in triumph. "My arrow struck home. I killed the Wolf!"

His huntsmen joined him at the river's edge. "Well done, Your Grace! Good shot!"

"I have rid the village of its cruel enemy!" he boasted. "My arrow found its mark, through Wolfie's heart!"

"Your Grace is a great hero," his men said. "We will go to the village and spread the good news. We will stop at the inn and drink to your health!"

Then one of the huntsmen limped up, minus his horse. "The stag got away," he complained. "I had him in my sights, but a foolish girl stood in my path. She frightened my horse and unseated me."

The others smiled and nodded. "A likely story!" they scoffed. "Tell the truth, Ralph. We know that the black mare was too spirited for you to handle. She threw you off and bolted, isn't that true?"

Huntsman Ralph hung his head in shame.

"But the Wolf is dead!" Duke Egbert puffed out his chest with pride. He twirled the ends of his moustache.

His men cheered and let him lead the

way out of the wood, across the meadow, back to the village in triumph.

Pearl lay in a deserted part of the wood.

The black mare's reins trailed along the ground. She gazed down in dismay. *The child is dead, thanks to my cruel rider.*

There was silence, except for the wind

whispering through the trees.

I will not return to the castle, the mare thought, her head drooping sadly. *I will not serve such masters, but live here in the wood.*

And so she trotted away from the place where Pearl lay. The wind sighed. No one passed by.

"Come quickly!" the squirrels said to Hans when they found him chopping wood with his father. "Red Riding-Hood needs your help!"

Hans put down his axe and wiped his hands. "What trouble is she in now? Has she lost her way in the wood while daydreaming as usual?"

"Worse!" the squirrels cried.

So Hans told his father that he was going to look for Red Riding-Hood and followed the squirrels to the clearing.

"What's this?" he frowned, when he saw the picnic scattered across the ground. The checked tablecloth had been trampled, the plates and knives stamped underfoot.

Rabbits jumped out of the undergrowth.

They gathered around Hans, their dark eyes troubled. "We were having a lovely picnic, but men came with bows and arrows. We ran for cover!"

"This is serious," Hans said with a frown. "Where is Red Riding-Hood? What happened to her?"

All the animals shook their heads. "We don't know," they admitted. "We ran away and left her. We're sorry, Hans, we were afraid."

Then the rat appeared from under a pile of dead leaves. "Yes," he said crossly. "We did what comes naturally. What chance does a rat or a rabbit or a squirrel have against a hail of arrows? And there were hounds baying for our blood. Of course we ran away!"

"I understand," Hans muttered. "But didn't anyone see what happened to Red Riding-Hood?"

"*Woo*-who knows?" the owl asked, swooping low across the clearing. "But we will find out if we search hard enough."

"Look here," Ratty said, pointing to the spot where a bow and arrow lay on the ground, half hidden by the tall grass.

Hans ran to pick up the arrow. He felt its sharp tip. Then he saw others embedded in the trees. "I wish I had come earlier. I heard the Duke and his men from afar. I should have been here to help."

"This is no time for regrets," Ratty insisted. "Let us look where the trail leads!"

"You're right." Hans took Ratty's advice.

He began to search the clearing.

"Here!" the rabbits and squirrels cried, scurrying ahead. "There are deep marks leading this way, as if a heavy weight has been dragged across the ground."

The Wolf breathed heavily. He lay beneath the willow roots, licking his wounds.

Shallow water lapped against his sweating sides. A trickle of blood ran down his shaggy neck.

Too close for comfort! he muttered. *Curse the Duke and his bow and arrow!*

Small grey fish swam around the tree's underwater roots. An otter watched the Wolf from the far bank.

Wolfie drew shallow breaths. His pink tongue lolled. *Soon!* he promised. "Soon I will leave my lair and seize my chance. Red Riding-Hood, watch out!"

The brown otter heard. She slipped silently into the river and swam. Only her blunt nose showed above the surface of the water as she made her way across the stream. Then she climbed out, shook herself and padded quietly into the wood.

8

The wind blew softly over Pearl's body. It lifted the golden-red curls from her forehead and blew against her cheeks.

The crack of dry twigs broke the deep silence of the wood.

Pearl's red cloak was ruffled by the wind. Her eyes were tight shut.

Something was approaching, then stopping to listen, then moving forward again. The creature was cautious and determined. It had spotted Pearl's bright red cloak. Now it came closer. And closer.

"I shouldn't be here, so far from the river!" the otter muttered. She hated the crisp feel of the fallen leaves under her webbed feet and the strange, dry-earth smells of the woodland.

A woodpecker high in the trees spotted her sleek body creeping stealthily towards the clearing. *Tap-tap-tock!* His beak drilled the bark. *Look up!*

"Be quiet!" the otter hissed. "I don't want anyone to know that I've left the riverbank!"

"Too late for that," the speckled woodpecker replied. "The kingfisher saw you and flew to tell me."

"Now half the world knows," the otter groaned. "And I only left the safety of the cool running water to pass on an important message about the Wolf."

"Tell me, *tock-tock*!"

"Can I trust you to pass on the message to all the animals in the wood so I can return to the river?" Why must the bird be so noisy, the otter wondered. It was all right for him – he could fly away from danger, whereas the four-footed creatures could only run and hide.

"Trust me!" The woodpecker cocked his head to one side.

"Then tell them that the Wolf lives." The otter

spoke slowly and carefully so that there could be no mistake.

Her news shocked the woodpecker. "Alive?" he echoed. "But the Duke is boasting that he aimed with his bow and arrow and shot the Wolf dead!"

"He lies," the otter insisted. "I saw Wolfie lying low by the old willow tree. Be sure to tell everyone, especially the child in the red cloak, for the Wolf plans to pounce and eat her up."

The woodpecker fluttered down from his branch. "I will tell the owl. We will spread the news," he promised.

"Good!" said the otter, relieved that her job was done. "Danger stalks this wood. Goodbye for now, Woodpecker, and good luck!"

*

Far away at the other edge of the wood, the stag raised his noble head. Distant sounds made him wary as he stepped between the trees.

Birds flew hither and thither. He heard faint human footsteps. But the child lay here on the ground without moving and he must find out what harm she had come to.

"Red Riding-Hood," he said softly. He had known it was her from her crimson cloak. It was the girl who had risked everything to save him, and now it was his turn to help her. "Open your eyes. Look up."

Pearl didn't move. Her face was pale.

The stag lowered his head. When he listened hard he could hear her light breaths. *Alive!* he thought with a sigh of relief. "Her spirit is strong. Let us hope that she will not die!"

The woodpecker flew to the owl and gave him the otter's message.

"*Woo*-Wolf!" the owl hooted through the trees. "Beware. The Wolf is alive!"

The squirrels heard and rushed along the branches, down the trunks to tell the rabbits, who hopped to the clearing to find Hans.

"Beware of the Wolf!" they cried.

Hans felt a flash of panic. If Red Riding-Hood was hurt and the Wolf found her before he did, that would be very bad news indeed. "We must follow this track!" he gasped. "See – the grass is flattened, there are horses' hooves deep in the soil."

"This way," Ratty insisted, scouting ahead. "The hoofprints are clear. They lead deep into the wood!"

Clumsily Hans trampled through bushes to follow the rat. Though he chopped logs for firewood and knew the paths well, he found he had never been this way before.

"Hurry!" Ratty said. Humans were slow and clumsy on their two legs, with ears that didn't hear and noses that didn't smell. "Listen!"

"What? I can't hear anything!" Hans was out of breath.

The rat tutted. "A deep, throaty cry – straight ahead. The stag is calling."

"He must have something to tell us,"

Hans decided quickly. "Go ahead. I"ll follow you!"

So Hans and the rat rushed on, followed by rabbits and squirrels, with the birds flying overhead.

Ratty ran swiftly. His feet pattered over stony ground, then through a shallow stream and up a hill until he came to the hillock which the stag had leaped earlier that afternoon. Beyond that he found the stag himself, standing guard over Red Riding-Hood.

The rat stopped in his tracks. Hans crashed through the bushes and almost tripped over him. Then, with a shock, he too saw Red Riding-Hood lying on the ground.

*

"Yoo-hoo, Farmer Meade!" It was late afternoon and Red Riding-Hood's grandmother was on her way home from work. It had been a tiring day. His Baby Grace had woken from his nap and cried for his rattle and his teddy bear. Her Grace the Duchess had flown off the handle because His Grace the Duke had rushed off to hunt as usual. Then news had come to the castle that the Duke had killed the Wolf and had stopped to celebrate at the village inn.

"Which put Her Grace in a terrible temper," Gran told Farmer Meade.

The old farmer had put his scythe over his shoulder and strode across the meadow to greet her. He'd asked her civilly how her day had been and the flood gates had opened.

"Her Grace went to the kitchen and took His Grace's supper from the cook and flung it into the pig pen. Then she took scissors to his hunting cloaks and cut them to shreds. As I left the castle, she was pouring his best wine down the drain."

"That's the type of woman to make a man's blood run cold," the farmer shuddered when Gran paused for breath. "Not like some I could mention."

"Why, Farmer Meade, whoever could you mean?" Gran smiled back. She took the old man's arm to climb the stile and together they entered the wood.

9

The wolf waited until the sun went down.

Watch and listen. Watch and listen.

The otter returned from the wood and slipped into the water, swimming silently to her home on the far bank.

Blue butterflies flitted through patches of sunlight and came to rest on purple

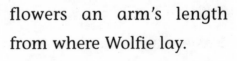

flowers an arm's length from where Wolfie lay.

78

The world is calm again, he thought. *The Duke drinks at the inn. Best of all – Red Riding-Hood has not left the wood!*

And so at last Wolfie stood up and shook himself dry, easing himself out of his lair.

"The Wolf is on the move!" the kingfisher flew like a blue arrow to tell the woodpecker, who tapped loudly at a tree trunk to bring the rabbits running.

"Raise the alarm!" the woodpecker said. "Our enemy, the Wolf, is on the prowl!"

Quickly the news passed through the wood.

"Where is Hans?" the squirrel who carried the news wondered.

"Who wants him?" Ratty demanded. He was on guard at the spot where Hans and the stag were tending Red Riding-Hood.

"We have news!" The squirrel's teeth chattered with fear. "Wolfie creeps through the wood, looking for his supper!"

"Nonsense!" Ratty retorted. He refused to believe idle gossip and still held to the version that suited him best. "The Wolf is dead. The Duke shot him. It's the first decent deed the man has done for years!"

"Not true!" the squirrel sighed. "The otter saw Wolfie lying low in his lair. And now the kingfisher says he is on the prowl!"

"We must believe it," the stag said, coming to join Ratty. Even he, with all his strength and magnificence, grew afraid. "Rat, can you think of a plan to lead the Wolf away from this spot?"

The rat thought hard. "Leave it to me," he said, scuttling through the bushes.

"Red Riding-Hood, you have to wake up!" Hans knelt beside Pearl. *Any moment now*, he thought, *she will open her eyes!*

But Pearl's head was locked in a dream world of blurred faces and whirling words, far away from the shadowy wood and the voice calling her.

Amber, is that you? Lily, why are you looking at me in that weird way? It's me – Pearl! Can't you hear me? Her head swam. She fought her way through tangled branches and roots and could not reach the light.

81

"How is she?" the stag asked Hans.

"Still asleep," Hans said sadly. "There's a big bruise on her forehead. She's been dragged here over a great distance. This is very bad. What can we do?"

"Keep the Wolf away for a start." The stag told Hans that brave Ratty had formed just such a plan. Then he listened again to Pearl's shallow breaths. "Bring water from the stream," he said.

So Hans ran and, taking off his neckerchief, he soaked it in cool, reviving liquid.

"Now dab her face," the stag instructed.

Pearl stirred as the cool cloth touched her cheek.

"Again," the stag murmured.

"O-o-oh!" Pearl sighed.

"Wake up!" Hans pleaded.

Pearl saw a faint patch of light ahead. Everything was blurred, but she thought she saw Hans's face – his grey eyes and fair curls – bending over her. And she heard his voice saying, "Wake up!"

Hans smiled as her eyelids fluttered open at last. "For goodness" sake, Red Riding-Hood, you took your time!"

"Where is everyone?" Wolfie wondered.

The wood was hushed. Even the evening songbirds were silent.

Ears pricked, yellow eyes gleaming, he stalked between the trees.

"Ah, good evening, Wolf!" a voice said from under a bush. Ratty strolled out. Though he seemed calm, his tiny heart was pounding.

"What's good about it?" Wolfie snarled, thinking that with one snap of his jaws he could gobble up this morsel. But rat was stringy and tough, and wasn't on his menu for tonight. "There's no time to talk. I want to eat."

"Quite. A big fellow like you needs to keep up his strength." Walking alongside the Wolf, Ratty carried on chatting. "What is it to be tonight? A nice young deer? A couple of succulent rabbits?"

"That's none of your business." Wolfie stopped to cast a suspicious glance at the rat. "Anyway, why do you ask?"

Ratty took a deep breath. He felt the fierce glare of the Wolf. He glimpsed his glistening teeth. *Don't tremble. Don't show your fear!* he reminded himself. "No reason," he said as calmly as he could.

"Aha!" Wolfie snapped. "I see why. You're hoping to join the feast!"

"Quite!" the rat said, thinking quickly and seizing his chance. "I know full well that your leftovers make a delicious meal for me!"

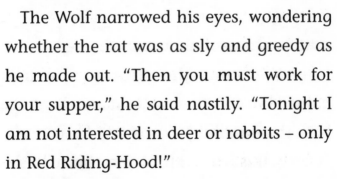

The Wolf narrowed his eyes, wondering whether the rat was as sly and greedy as he made out. "Then you must work for your supper," he said nastily. "Tonight I am not interested in deer or rabbits – only in Red Riding-Hood!"

"Quite!" Ratty jumped in again. He set the trap for the Wolf to fall into. "The girl is a very good choice, sir. What is it that you would you like me to do?"

Wolfie still stared narrowly at the rat. He was silent for a long time. When he spoke, his voice sounded like the hiss of a snake. "Show me where she is!"

A shiver ran down the rat's spine and he swallowed hard. "With pleasure, Wolf."

"Take me to the place!"

"Only too pleased."

"Now!"

Ratty's pounding heart steadied as he turned towards the clearing. He had gained Wolfie's trust and intended to trick him thoroughly. "Certainly!" he gushed. "Come this way. Mind the thorn bush. Take care not to trip over the boulder to your left. That's right, sir – follow me!"

10

"Can you sit up?" the stag asked Pearl kindly. He was glad that the child was awake, but knew they must move her out of the wood before the Wolf found her. "Can you stand?"

"Whoa!" Pearl said, putting her hand to her forehead as she got to her feet. "Ouch, that hurts!"

"I'm not surprised," Hans muttered.

"You've a bump as big as a goose egg!"

"I feel dizzy," Pearl said weakly.

"Climb on my back and I will carry you away from danger," the stag advised.

"What danger?" Pearl asked woozily. Things were only slowly coming back to her – she recalled making sandwiches, packing the picnic box, setting out for the clearing in the wood.

Hans clicked his tongue impatiently. "Remember Wolfie?"

Ah yes, the wolf! And arrows whizzing between the trees. A reckless rider on a black mare . . . "Scary!" she whispered.

"Help her up," the stag told Hans. "Who knows if the rat's plan succeeded, or if the Wolf is on our trail?"

So Hans lifted Pearl on to the stag's

broad back. "Don't fall off," he warned. "You have enough bruises for one day."

"Ouch!" Pearl groaned. Her legs ached, her back was stiff, there was a pain in her ribs. "Ouch! Ouch!"

"Come!" the stag said, taking his first slow steps through the wood. "We must get you home to your mother before nightfall."

"I'll be honest with you, Farmer Meade." Gran gossiped non-stop on the path through the wood to her house by the old mill. She didn't even pause for breath.

"Life at the castle is not what you might expect. His Baby Grace is a delight, but the Duchess has a mean temper and must not be crossed. Besides, she is vain beyond belief. She believes herself to be more beautiful than in plain fact she is . . ."

The farmer leaned his scythe against a tree and gave Gran his hand to climb over a fallen branch. "Let me carry your basket," he offered. "Wait. Let me help you across this stream."

"Why, thank you, Farmer Meade!" Gran blushed as the old man caught her around her stout waist. "I'm later than I intended coming home today. The shadows are lengthening, but I feel quite safe with you by my side."

"Here is the clearing, straight ahead,"

the farmer comforted. "We will stop a while and rest, if that suits you."

Gran smiled and blushed some more. "It suits me very well," she sighed.

"Are you certain that this is the way?" the Wolf snapped at the rat. "I see no sign of Red Riding-Hood, I smell no scent!"

"I'm certain as can be," Ratty replied, his heart in his mouth. What would happen when they reached the clearing and Wolfie found he had been tricked? *Better have another plan ready for that nasty moment*, he thought.

"Isn't this where she had her foolish picnic?" Wolfie overtook the rat as he spied the checked tablecloth trampled in the grass and the basket lying open at the base of a tree.

"You are right," Ratty said, scurrying to keep up. The Wolf's stride was long, his patience short. "The Duke and his hunters took the picnickers by surprise. And you too, if I'm not mistaken."

"So where is Red Riding-Hood now?" The Wolf stopped at the edge of the clearing and hid behind a tree. Every hair bristled, and his bushy tail twitched.

"Right here," Ratty said faintly. His trick had worked, but now the game was up. *Be prepared to scarper*, he told himself. *Ready, steady . . .* "At least she was, the last time I saw her." *Go!*

Wolfie glared at the empty clearing. He bared his teeth and gave a deep growl. "Rat, you're a fool and will pay for this!"

But when the Wolf turned his head, Ratty was gone.

"And the Duke," Gran gossiped. "He is, as they say, a fine figure of a man, but his heart is selfish and cold. Why, he thinks more about waxing his moustache in front of the mirror than spending time with his own dear Baby Grace!"

"Tut-tut!" Farmer Meade said. "Here we are in the clearing. And here is a nice log to sit upon!"

"Better than nothing," Wolfie said from his hiding place behind the tree. He watched the old man and woman sit on a log. "They would make easy prey and a fine supper if all else fails!"

But wait! The old woman had spotted the ruins of the picnic and jumped up from the log.

"Oh, my!" Gran cried. "This is my granddaughter's picnic basket, and all her plates and knives are scattered across the clearing!"

"You're right. I saw Red Riding-Hood carry the hamper across the meadow," the farmer said. "What's been going on here?"

"Something's not right."

Looking all around, Gran failed to see Wolfie behind the tree. "The child wouldn't run off and leave this mess unless something bad had happened!"

"Hmmmm." Wolfie crouched and licked his lips. What would be the harm of pouncing here and now? With the grandmother as main course, Red Riding-Hood would still be available for pudding!

"Hold tight," the stag told Pearl. He ran on ahead of Hans, carrying her on his back. "Tell me if I go too fast."

"No, I'm OK," Pearl insisted, though she ached all over. "Mum will be worried about me. We'd better hurry."

"When we reach the village you must wait for Hans and walk the final steps with him," the stag warned as he made out the clearing ahead. "The Duke may still be at the inn and I dare not carry you to the cottage door."

"Fine," she assured him, clinging tight to his neck. "You've done so much for me,

I can't thank you enough."

"But wait!" Suddenly the stag saw Gran running frantically around the clearing, picking up the ruins of Pearl's picnic. "Help is at hand," he told Pearl.

And Stag strode ahead into the clearing and stood in full view of the hidden Wolf, raising his head and calling to the humans in his deep voice.

"Stop!" Ratty called from the branch of a nearby tree. "Turn around, Stag. Go back. Do not proceed!"

But it was too late. Wolfie's wildest dream had come true. The stag and Red Riding-Hood had walked carelessly into view. Here was a whole feast – starter, main course and dessert!

"Beware the Wolf!" Farmer Meade cried

as he saw the creature leap out from behind the tree.

"Get away, you horrible beast!" Gran yelled, shaking her fists at the shaggy, snarling creature.

The stag stood still as stone. "Climb down," he told Pearl. "Stay here and wait for Hans. Don't move."

Pearl did as she was told. She felt too weak to act as she watched the Wolf rush at Gran, his teeth bared. Farmer Meade quickly stepped in front of Gran to shield her from Wolfie's fangs, then the stag lowered his head and charged.

Three against one! And now Hans came running through the wood, took in what was happening and raced to help. "Surround the Wolf!" he cried. "Make a circle. Don't let him escape!"

Gran rolled up her sleeves. Farmer Meade advanced. The stag stood his ground.

"Watch out, Wolfie's about to pounce!" Pearl cried.

He snarled and crouched low. His mouth watered. Supper was the snap of his jaws away. Grandmamma was his dish of choice!

"Oh no you don't!" she cried, looking Wolfie in the eye. She spotted the farmer's scythe propped against the nearest tree and reached out to snatch it.

Wolfie saw the glittering blade as Gran raised it above her head.

"Go, Gran!" Pearl yelled.

Gran swiped the blade towards the Wolf's head. But Wolfie was quick. He leaped to one side. Gran missed. The Wolf hit his head against the tree and saw stars.

"Again!" Hans cried as the stag and Farmer Meade closed in.

Gran raised the scythe a second time. "I"ll get you, you sneaking, sly creature!"

The dizzy Wolf was slower this time. Still he managed to dodge as the blade came down. He twisted sideways, scrambling to one side of the tree and whirling round to turn his back on the enemy.

A third time Gran lifted the scythe and brought it down. *Whizz-clunk!* The blade was embedded in the trunk.

And Wolfie was getting away, making a run for the riverbank, counting his blessings and knowing that he was lucky to be alive and in one piece . . . almost! When he glanced over his shoulder, he saw that there was one small part of himself missing.

"So near yet so far!" Hans gasped, stooping to pick up the white tip of Wolfie's tail. "It seems the Wolf lives to fight another day."

11

"That's the last time I let you go into the woods alone!" Red Riding-Hood's mother declared. "I was worried sick when you didn't get back by sunset."

"Don't be so hard on her," Hans pleaded. "She's had a bad scare."

"Which is exactly my point. That's why I don't want you going off all by yourself."

Pearl sat patiently as her mother fussed

and fretted. She remembered sadly how she'd said goodbye to Stag at the edge of the wood then smiled to herself at how eager Farmer Meade had been to take Gran all the way home to her cottage by the mill.

"I'm fine," she insisted, though her head still throbbed. "No need to worry. Gran chased the Wolf away."

"But what if your grandmother hadn't been there?" her mother asked.

"Then Hans was close by. He would have come to the rescue. *And Stag, and Ratty, and the otter, the squirrels, the rabbits* . . . But she didn't tell her mother that part of the story.

"Look here – I got the tip of Wolfie's tail!" Hans held up his trophy for all to admire. "See this, Hannah?"

Red Riding-Hood's young cousin sat on a stool by the fire, eating a supper of leftover scones and cookies. She wrinkled her nose. "Yuck, horrid!" she declared as Hans wafted the furry object under her nose.

"How long will you be here?" Hans asked, pulling up another stool and launching into a long chat. "How come you're staying with your aunt?"

Yeah, how long do I have to share my room? Pearl wondered with a frown. It didn't help that Hannah had golden curls and was mega pretty. Probably spoiled rotten too.

"Red Riding-Hood!" Her mother broke into her sulky thoughts. "Did you hear me? I asked you to take the hamper upstairs, out of the way. Remember, no more picnics for you!"

"OK," Pearl sighed, squeezing past her cousin. *That's all right, Hannah – don't move. I can manage!*

Trudge, trudge up the stairs and still sulking. Head hurting. Bending down to put the hamper under her bed. Feeling dizzy. Seeing a dim light growing brighter.

"It's about time Pearl was back," Amber said, looking at her watch. "If she doesn't hurry we'll have to go to the supermarket without her."

"Yeah, and face some awkward questions from your mum," Lily pointed out. "Like, 'Where's Pearl?' and 'Why didn't you tell me she'd gone home?'"

Amber went to the window and looked out. "Come back, Pearl!"

Whoosh! The basement door flew open and the room filled with sparkling light.

"Magic!" Lily laughed. "How cool is that!"

"So?" Amber hissed. She sat in the middle of the back seat, with Pearl and Lily on either side. Her mum had stopped at traffic lights, turning up the volume on the CD player. "What happened this time?"

"Yeah, how did you get that bump on your head?" Lily wanted to know. They hadn't had time to find out. As soon as Pearl had been suddenly whooshed back to the basement, Amber's mum had whisked them all off to the supermarket.

"Not now. I'll tell you later," Pearl sighed. She was so-o-o tired after her hard day and – yes, she had to admit she was still sulking about Hannah.

"Now!" Amber refused to be fobbed off. "Give us the gory details. Tell us about Wolfie!"

"And the rat," Lily reminded her. "Come on, Pearl. What's up?"

"Hannah is what's up," Pearl admitted as the lights turned green and she began to tell Amber and Lily what they were dying to know. "I mean, nobody asked me if she could share my room, did they? She's a cousin I didn't even know I had, and now she's moved in."

"Will she still be there next time you're whooshed?" Amber wondered.

Pearl sighed as they joined the queue for the supermarket car park. "Who knows?" she muttered. "But I definitely, totally, *so-o* hope she's not!"

COLOURING FUN!

Carefully colour the Dressing-Up Dreams picture
on the next page and then send it in to us.

Or you can draw your very own fairytale
character. You might want to think about what
they would wear or if they have special powers.

Each month, we will put the best entries
on the website gallery and one lucky winner
will receive a magical Dressing-Up Dreams
goodie bag!

Send your drawing,
your name, age and address on a postcard to:
Pearl's Dressing-Up Dreams Competition

UK Readers:	**Australian Readers:**	**New Zealand Readers:**
Hodder Children's Books	Hachette Children's Books	Hachette Livre NZ Ltd
338 Euston Road	Level 17/207 Kent Street	PO Box 100 749
London NW1 3BH	Sydney NSW 2000	North Shore City 0745
kidsmarketing@hodder.co.uk	childrens.books@hachette.com.au	childrensbooks@hachette.co.r

Have you checked out...

www.dressingupdreams.net

It's the place to go for games, downloads, activities, sneak previews and lots of fun!

You'll find a special dressing-up game and lots of activities and fun things to do, as well as news on Dressing-Up Dreams and all your favourite characters.

Sign up to the newsletter at **www.dressingupdreams.net** to receive extra clothes for your Dressing-Up Dreams doll and the opportunity to enter special members only competitions.

What happens next...?
Log onto www.dressingupdreams.net for a sneak preview of my next adventure!

WIN A *Dressing-Up Dreams* GOODIE BAG!

CAN YOU SPOT THE TWO DIFFERENCES AND THE HIDDEN LETTER IN THESE TWO PICTURES OF PEARL?

There is a spot-the-difference picture and hidden letter in the back of all four Dressing-Up Dreams books about Pearl (look for the books with 9 to 12 on the spine). Hidden in one of the pictures above is a secret letter. Find all four letters and put them together to make a special Dressing-Up Dreams word, then send it to us. Each month, we will put the correct entries in a draw and one lucky winner will receive a magical Dressing-Up Dreams goodie bag including an exclusive Dressing-Up Dreams keyring!

Send your magical word, your name, age and your address on a postcard to: **Pearl's Dressing-Up Dreams Competition**

UK Readers:
Hodder Children's Books
338 Euston Road
London NW1 3BH
idsmarketing@hodder.co.uk

Australian Readers:
Hachette Children's Books
Level 17/207 Kent Street
Sydney NSW 2000
childrens.books@hachette.com.au

New Zealand Readers:
Hachette Livre NZ Ltd
PO Box 100 749
North Shore City 0745
childrensbooks@hachette.co.n

Only one entry per child. Final draw: 30th March 2010
For full terms and conditions go to http://www.hodderchildrens.co.uk/Terms_and_Conditions.htm